November 8, 1993

To.

Christine

1st Birthday

Happy Birthday!

Love Aunt Ginney, Uncle Fred.
Fred, Jason & Nick

minnie 'n me

NO FAIR PEEKING

BY Sara Parke

ILLUSTRATED BY Vaccaro Associates

Disney PRESS

NEW YORK

Minnie 'n Me: No Fair Peeking
is published by Disney Press,
a subsidiary of The Walt Disney Company,
500 South Buena Vista Street,
Burbank, California 91521.
The story and art herein are copyright © 1991
The Walt Disney Company.
No part of this book may be printed
or reproduced in any manner whatsoever,
whether mechanical or electronic,
without the written permission of the publisher.
The stories, characters or incidents
in this publication are entirely fictional.

Published by Disney Press
114 Fifth Avenue
New York, New York 10011

Printed in the U.S.A.
ISBN 1-56282-037-0
8 7 6 5 4 3 2 1

This book is dedicated to

Paste your
photo here

Every day after school Penny and Daisy knew where to find Minnie. She would be sitting under a tree, writing in her diary.

"Ever since you got that diary for your birthday," Daisy said, "we have to wait for you to play!"

"Just one more minute," said Minnie, "and I'll be right there."

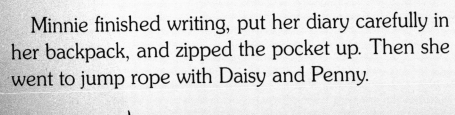

Minnie finished writing, put her diary carefully in her backpack, and zipped the pocket up. Then she went to jump rope with Daisy and Penny.

Penny asked Minnie, "What do you write in that book, anyway?"

Minnie smiled. "Just stuff," she said. "Poems. Things I think about."

"What things?" asked Daisy.

"Oh, just things," answered Minnie.

The girls walked over to Minnie's house for a
snack. While Minnie went to make peanut butter and
banana sandwiches, Penny and Daisy waited in
Minnie's bedroom.

"I wonder what Minnie writes in her diary," Penny said.

"So do I!" said Daisy. "Do you think she writes about us?"

Penny opened Minnie's backpack and took out the diary.
"Look, Daisy," she said, "it doesn't say 'Private' on the cover."

"That doesn't matter," said Daisy. "We shouldn't read it."

"I suppose not," said Penny. And she put the diary back.

"Wait," said Daisy. "Minnie never told us we *couldn't*
read her diary."

"And if we do it fast," Penny added, "she'll never find out."

Penny picked up Minnie's diary again. She turned
to the first page and read, "'Today I got the prettiest
birthday card from Penny and Daisy. I can't wait
until their birthdays. I'm going to give them each a
surprise party. I know we'll be best friends forever!'"

Page after page, Daisy and Penny read the nice things Minnie had to say about them. Then they turned to the last entry in the book.

"Listen to this!" Daisy cried. She grabbed the book away from Penny. "'They make so much noise I can hardly stand it,'" she read. "'Sometimes I wish they would go away!'"

"I guess Minnie means us," Penny said, sadly. "She didn't really mean the part about our being best friends forever."

"Well, if that's how Minnie feels," said Daisy, "we *will* go away!" She put the diary back in Minnie's backpack.

Just then Minnie came back with sandwiches and milk. Daisy and Penny hurried toward the door. "We're not hungry," said Daisy.

"But a few minutes ago you said you were!" said Minnie.

"Well, we have to go now," said Penny, and she and Daisy rushed out.

Minnie got her diary and wrote, "How strange! We were having fun, but then Daisy and Penny left in a hurry. I wonder why."

The first thing Minnie did the next morning was call Daisy.

"Do you want to come over?" Minnie asked.

"No," said Daisy. "I'm busy today." And she hung up.

"I know something's wrong," thought Minnie. "We always spend Saturday together."

Minnie went over to Penny's house. Penny's aunt answered the door. "Hello, Minnie," she said. "I didn't think I'd see you over here today."

"Why not?" asked Minnie. "Isn't Penny here?"

"No, dear. She's over at Daisy's."

Minnie stepped back. Why hadn't she been invited?

As soon as she got to school on Monday, Minnie
hurried over to Daisy. But when Daisy saw Minnie,
she turned and walked the other way.

Then Minnie ran into Penny in the lunchroom.
"Penny, I need to ask you something," said
Minnie.
"Sorry, Minnie, not now," said Penny. "Daisy and I
are having lunch with some other friends."

Minnie tried not to cry. She found an empty table
and ate lunch all by herself.

After school Minnie sat under her tree, writing in her diary, while Daisy and Penny played ball together.

"I don't know why Penny and Daisy won't talk to me," Minnie wrote. "What did I do wrong?"

Suddenly a ball rolled next to Minnie. Daisy and
Penny came running after it. Minnie grabbed the ball
and said, "I'm not going to give it back until you tell
me what's going on."

"Why should we?" said Penny, crossing her arms. "*You* never tell *us* anything! You write everything in your dumb diary. And you know what? We would never throw *you* a surprise party!"

Penny clapped her hand over her mouth.

"How did you know I was planning to throw you a party?" Minnie asked, angrily. "Did you and Daisy read my diary?"

"Yes!" said Daisy. "And I'm glad we did. Now we know how you really feel about us!"

"What do you mean?" demanded Minnie. "You two are my best friends."

"That's not true," said Penny. "I read what you wrote myself!"

"Show me!" said Minnie. She held out her diary.

"Here," said Penny. "It's this part." And she read it out loud.

Daisy and Penny stared at Minnie. Daisy cried,
"We couldn't believe you would write that about us!"
"But I didn't," said Minnie, slowly. "I was writing
about the birds outside my window. They were
making so much noise I couldn't sleep!"

"Oh..." said Daisy, blushing.

"Oh, no!" said Penny. "We made a huge mistake."

"That's right," said Minnie. "And even if I had written something mean, maybe it was because I was in a bad mood, or we'd had a stupid fight. Anyway, you shouldn't have read my diary without asking. It's private!"

"You're right, Minnie," said Daisy. "We never should have read your diary. If we'd left it alone, no one's feelings would have been hurt."

Penny nodded solemnly. "We're sorry, Minnie."

Minnie gave the ball back to Penny. "I forgive
you," she said. "Just promise you won't ever snoop
again."

"We promise!" said Daisy and Penny.

The next day after school Minnie had a surprise
for Penny and Daisy. It was a diary for each of them!

"Thanks, Minnie," said Daisy, hugging hers to her
chest.

"I'm going to start writing in mine right now!" said
Penny.

So the three girls sat under the tree together and
began to write.